POST CARD

W9-ALV-519

POST CARD

POST CARD

Post Card

USA FIRST-CLASS FOREVER

THIS IS A BORZOI BOOK PUBLISHED BY ALFRED A. KNOPF

Text copyright © 2016 by Jen Arena. Jacket art and interior illustrations copyright © 2016 by Matt Hunt. All rights reserved.
Published in the United States by Alfred A. Knopf, an imprint of Random House Children's Books, a division of
Penguin Random House LLC, New York. Knopf, Borzoi Books, and the colophon are registered trademarks of Penguin Random House LLC.
Visit us on the Web! randomhousekids.com
Educators and librarians, for a variety of teaching tools, visit us at RHTeachersLibrarians.com
Image on page 36 courtesy of the Library of Congress
Library of Congress Cataloging-in-Publication Data
Arena, Jen.   Lady Liberty's holiday / by Jennifer Arena ; illustrated by Matt Hunt. — First edition.   p.   cm.
Summary: When the Statue of Liberty decides she wants to see more of America, she leaves her post in New York to explore.
ISBN 978-0-553-52067-5 (trade) — ISBN 978-0-553-52068-2 (lib. bdg.) — ISBN 978-0-553-52069-9 (ebook)
1. Statue of Liberty (New York, N.Y.)—Juvenile fiction. [1. Statue of Liberty (New York, N.Y.)—Fiction. 2. Vacations—Fiction.
3. Voyages and travels—Fiction. 4. United States—Fiction.] I. Hunt, Matt, illustrator. II. Title.
PZ7.1.A74Lad 2016   [E]—dc23   2014038892
The text of this book is set in 24-point Fling a Ling Medium.
The illustrations were created using a mixture of traditional and digital pencil and paint.
MANUFACTURED IN CHINA   May 2016   10 9 8 7 6 5 4 3 2 1   First Edition
Random House Children's Books supports the First Amendment and celebrates the right to read.

For Halina, Gus, and Alex
— J.A.

For my family
— M.H.

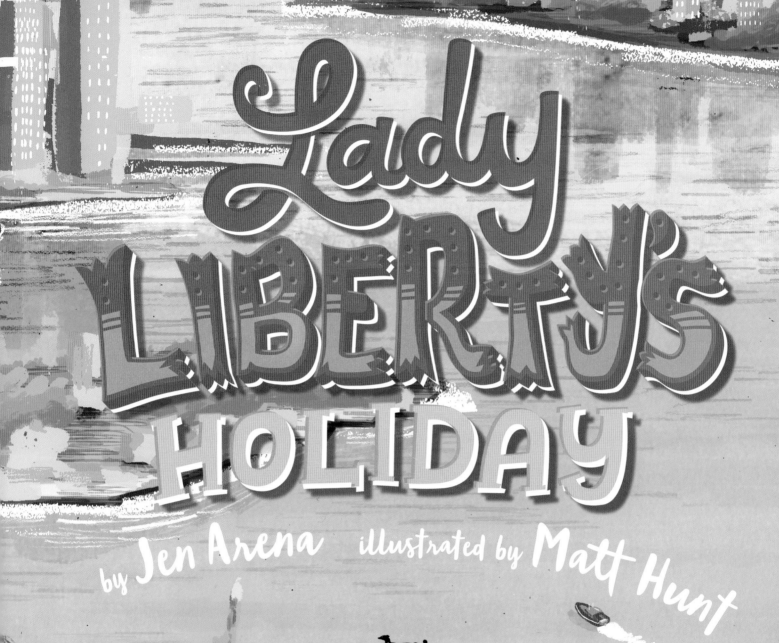

Lady Liberty's Holiday

by Jen Arena   illustrated by Matt Hunt

Alfred A. Knopf
New York

Not long before the Fourth of July, Lady Liberty
woke up feeling a little blue . . . despite being green.
Year after year, she stood by New York Harbor,
a torch in one hand, a tablet in the other.

"Moe, every day feels the same," Liberty said. "I see the same skyscrapers, the same city. My neck is stiff. My arms are aching. I've had a cramp in my leg for a decade at least."

Moe puffed out his pigeon chest. "Lady, you need a getaway!" he told her. "Go and see the country! Shake the rust off and—"

"I don't have any rust!" Lady Liberty protested.

Moe went on, "Give yourself a holiday!"

Moe's words echoed in Liberty's head. She had seen only one little corner of America. What was the rest like?

That night, she lowered her torch. She put down her tablet. She pried her sandals from the stone, and then . . .

the Statue of Liberty
snuck away!

First she left footprints on the Jersey Shore . . .

and built the biggest sand castle Cape Cod had ever seen.

She washed the sand off at Niagara Falls.

Then Lady Liberty
headed west.

She watched the
Mississippi River from the top
of the St. Louis Arch . . .

and in Kansas,
wheat fields
tickled her feet.

She even did some sightseeing in South Dakota.

She hiked across the Rocky Mountains . . .

in sandals.

Afterward, the California sunshine made her so
sleepy, she napped on the Golden Gate Bridge.

Back in New York, Moe was starting to worry.
The Fourth of July was three days away, but without
Lady Liberty, people weren't in a holiday mood.

Tourists were gloomy.

Cops were cross.

Even the stock market
was down.

The New York Times
PANIC AS STOCKS CRASH!
SHOCK

The mayor was talking about canceling the Fourth of July!

"What if Liberty doesn't come back in time?" Moe said. "What if she's gone for good?"

He had to find her!

It was true. Liberty wasn't thinking of returning.
At the Grand Canyon, for once in her life, Lady Liberty felt small.

She trekked through a hot, dry desert and slurped water from a Yellowstone geyser.

It tasted awful.

Deep in the heart of Texas, she napped under the big, bright stars with cattle all around.

She danced to music
near New Orleans,

used the Florida Keys
as stepping-stones,

and waded through
Southern swamps.

Lady Liberty was shaking an alligator off her big toe
when she heard the familiar flap of pigeon wings.
It was Moe!

He perched on her shoulder. "Lady,
I've been looking all over for you," he said.
"You have?" Liberty asked. "How are
things in New York?"
"Not so good," Moe said. "They're
canceling the Fourth of July."

Liberty bolted up as if she'd been struck by lightning. "Canceling the Fourth of July? They can't!"

Moe nodded. "Nobody feels like celebrating without you."

"But the Fourth of July isn't about *me*. It's about America!" Liberty cried. "I've seen this country. The purple mountains, the shining seas, the bridges and buildings. Everyone should know how amazing it is and celebrate it!"

Moe fluffed his feathers. "Come back to New York," he said. "The mayor might change his mind—" He didn't get to finish.

Liberty was already running north.

At dawn, the sun shone on the copper dress of
Lady Liberty in New York Harbor, where she had stood
for over a hundred years. That night, fireworks lit the sky,
and people waved flags, sang songs, and shouted,

"Happy Fourth of July!"

And Liberty was blue no longer.

"It was good to get away," she told Moe.

"But it's great to be home."

⋆ Lady Liberty's Story ⋆

The Statue of Liberty is as American as apple pie, but her story begins in France.

In 1865, a sculptor named Frédéric-Auguste Bartholdi went to a dinner at the home of Édouard René de Laboulaye. Laboulaye was a big admirer of America. At the time, France was ruled by Emperor Napoleon III. America, on the other hand, wasn't governed by an emperor or a king, but by elected representatives. Laboulaye hoped someday his country would have a similar system of government, but in other ways he felt America and France were already alike. After all, both countries believed in liberty and equality. At that dinner, Laboulaye proposed building a monument to bring the two countries closer together. This suggestion stayed with Bartholdi. He even had an idea for the monument—a large statue of a woman holding up a light.

Laboulaye and Bartholdi wanted the statue to be ready for America's centennial in 1876, but they missed that date by a decade. It was a complicated project! For one thing, Bartholdi and Leboulaye had to raise money to pay for the statue. From the beginning, they pictured the monument as a gift from the French people to the American people. France would pay for the statue. America would pay for the base. Bartholdi traveled to America, but he had trouble getting people interested. Even after the statue was finished in Paris, dismantled bolt by bolt and copper sheet by copper sheet, packed into 214 crates, and shipped across the ocean in May 1885, America *still* hadn't raised the money to build the base. That was when Joseph Pulitzer, the publisher of a popular newspaper called *The World,* got involved. He promised to print the name of everyone who gave money—any amount, no matter how small—in his newspaper. Schoolchildren sent in pennies. Rich men sent much more, and eventually over $100,000 was raised.

Building the statue was very complicated, too. Bartholdi started with a plaster model only 4.5 feet tall. He scaled that up several times to reach the statue's final height of 151 feet and one inch. After making wooden molds in the shape of the statue, workers hammered thin copper sheets—only 3/32 of an inch thick!—around the molds and then riveted them together on an iron framework. Meanwhile, Gustave Eiffel, the same man who built the Eiffel Tower, designed a metal skeleton to support Bartholdi's hollow statue, in even the worst weather.

On his first trip to America, Bartholdi found the perfect spot for the Statue of Liberty—Bedloe's Island, at the entrance to New York Harbor. While the statue had started as a way to highlight a friendship between two countries, over time she stood for much more. Because of where she was placed, she became a symbol of freedom to immigrants arriving in America. To many of them, Lady Liberty represented the new life they would have there. In 1903, a poem by Emma Lazarus was added to the pedestal to honor the immigrants. "Give me your tired, your poor, / Your huddled masses yearning to breathe free" are its most famous lines.

The Statue of Liberty was unveiled on October 28, 1886. A huge parade marched down Fifth Avenue to the tip of Manhattan. Bands played both the French and American national anthems. Even Grover Cleveland, the president of the United States, came to welcome Lady Liberty. When Bartholdi pulled a rope to remove the French flag covering the statue's copper face, America got its first glimpse of Lady Liberty . . . and Lady Liberty got her first glimpse of America.

★ Secrets of the Statue of Liberty ★

Some people say Bartholdi based Liberty's face on his mother's.

Liberty's arm was displayed in America for six years. During part of that time, her head was shown in Paris.

By the time the statue was unveiled, Laboulaye had passed away. He died in 1883.

Visitors can climb a staircase inside the Statue of Liberty to her crown.

There's a secret entrance to the Statue of Liberty in her right foot. That's how the workers entered the statue during construction.

Lady Liberty's nose is 4 feet 6 inches long.

Liberty looks green now, but when she was built, her copper skin was the color of a new penny. As the copper weathered, it changed color, getting what is called a patina. By around 1915, the statue was completely green.

Liberty has seven spikes on her crown—one for each of the seven continents or seven seas.

Liberty's tablet says, "July IV MDCCLXXVI," or July 4, 1776.

Bedloe's Island was renamed Liberty Island in 1956 after its famous monument.

Lightning strikes the Statue of Liberty hundreds of times every year.

To learn more about the Statue of Liberty, you can read these books:

Curlee, Lynn. *Liberty.* New York: Atheneum Books for Young Readers, 2000.

Deitz Shea, Pegi. *Liberty Rising: The Story of the Statue of Liberty.* New York: Henry Holt, 2005.

Hochain, Serge. *Building Liberty: A Statue Is Born.* Translated by Camilla Bozzoli. Washington, DC: National Geographic Society, 2004.

Malam, John. *You Wouldn't Want to Be a Worker on the Statue of Liberty! A Monument You'd Rather Not Build.* Brighton, UK: Salariya Book Company, 2008.

Mann, Elizabeth. *Statue of Liberty.* New York: Mikaya Press, Inc., 2011.

Rappaport, Doreen. *Lady Liberty: A Biography.* Somerville, MA: Candlewick, 2008.